SO-AXC-737

OTHER YEARLING BOOKS YOU WILL ENJOY:

HAPPY BIRTHDAY, MOLE AND TROLL, *Tony Johnston*
NIGHT NOISES AND OTHER MOLE AND TROLL STORIES,
 Tony Johnston
MOLE AND TROLL TRIM THE TREE, *Tony Johnston*
"BEE MY VALENTINE!", *Miriam Cohen*
FIRST GRADE TAKES A TEST, *Miriam Cohen*
JIM'S DOG MUFFINS, *Miriam Cohen*
LOST IN THE MUSEUM, *Miriam Cohen*
NO GOOD IN ART, *Miriam Cohen*
WHEN WILL I READ?, *Miriam Cohen*
IT'S GEORGE!, *Miriam Cohen*

YEARLING BOOKS/YOUNG YEARLINGS/YEARLING CLASSICS are
designed especially to entertain and enlighten young peo-
ple. Patricia Reilly Giff, consultant to this series, received
the bachelor's degree from Marymount College. She holds
the master's degree in history from St. John's University, and
a Professional Diploma in Reading from Hofstra University.
She was a teacher and reading consultant for many years,
and is the author of numerous books for young readers.

For a complete listing of all Yearling titles, write to
Dell Readers Service, P.O. Box 1045,
South Holland, IL 60473.

DEPARTMENT OF INSTRUCTION
MOUNTAIN VIEW SCHOOL DISTRICT

the adventures of
Mole and Troll

by
Tony Johnston

Illustrated by
Wallace Tripp

A YOUNG YEARLING BOOK

Published by
Dell Publishing
a division of
Bantam Doubleday Dell Publishing Group, Inc.
666 Fifth Avenue
New York, New York 10103

Text copyright © 1972 by Tony Johnston
Illustrations copyright © 1972 by Wallace Tripp

ISBN: 0-440-40218-2

Reprinted by arrangement with The Putnam & Grosset Group

Printed in the United States of America

August 1989

10 9 8 7 6 5 4 3 2 1

W

MOTHER'S DAY

One afternoon Troll was lying in his
hammock looking worried.
Mole came to visit.
"You look worried," he said.

5

"I am," said Troll. "Today is Mother's Day, and I do not have a gift for my grandmother."

"But, Troll," said Mole, "if it is Mother's Day, you do not need a gift for your grandmother. You can wait till Grandmother's Day."

"Dear Mole," said Troll, "if I feel like giving my grandmother a gift, I can give it whenever I want. Besides, there is no Grandmother's Day."

"There should be," said Mole.

"Well, there isn't," said Troll. "Now please help me think of a gift."

They tried hard to think of a gift for Troll's grandmother.

Suddenly Troll got very excited.

"I know just what my grandmother
would like!" he cried.

"What?"

"A new dress."

"That is a good idea," said Mole.

"No, it isn't," said Troll, getting worried
again.

"But why?" asked Mole.

"I need a model. I need someone to try it
on for size."

"Then I volunteer," said Mole. "Try your
grandmother's dress on me."

"What a good friend you are," said Troll.
"That is a big help."

Troll took out some flowered chintz he
had been saving. He took out a big silver
needle. He took out a big silver thimble.
He took out some big silver scissors. He
took out lots of silver pins. And he made
a dress for his grandmother.

Mole was a good model. He did not
wiggle.
Troll was a good sewer. He did not poke
his fingers.

Soon the dress was finished. It had white
laces down the front, puffy sleeves, and
flowers all over. Mole tried it on. It fit
perfectly.

Troll was ironing the dress and humming
a little song.
Outside someone was humming too and
coming up the path.
Troll looked to see who it was.
"Oh, Mole!" he cried. "I have made a
BIG mistake!"

"What mistake?" asked Mole.
"Grandmother is outside humming and
coming up the path, and she is not
anything like you! She is one mole taller
and three moles fatter! Now I have
nothing for her but a too-tight dress!"

13

"Your garden is full of flowers," said
Mole. "You can give her a spring bouquet
instead."

"What a fine idea!" said Troll. He ran
outside and picked a lovely spring
bouquet.

Troll's grandmother smelled the flowers
deeply. She was very happy. She gave
Troll a big hug and went home humming
louder than ever.

"Troll?" asked Mole. "What about the dress? You worked hard to make it. Now it is wasted."

"It is not wasted," said Troll. "It is just your size. It is just your color. I will give it to you."

"But, Troll," said Mole, "I do not wear dresses."

Troll looked sad.

"But I know someone who needs a new
dress," said Mole.

"Who?" asked Troll.

"My scarecrow," said Mole. "To keep the
birds away."

So they put the dress on the scarecrow.

17

The birds were *really* scared of that. Troll
was happy. The dress looked very pretty,
blowing in the breeze. Mole was happy,
too. His garden grew taller than he was.

THE BEACH

Mole and Troll went to the beach. They
felt the warm sand between their toes.
They felt the warm sun on their backs.
When it got too hot, they sat by the tide
pools and dangled their toes in the water.

Suddenly Mole jumped up.

"You pinched me!" he shrieked.

"I did not," said Troll. "I was sitting here dangling my toes and minding my own business."

"Well, maybe your business is pinching,"
said Mole. "There is no one else around."
Troll made a face. He did not like being
called a pincher.
No one said anything for a little while.

Then Troll felt a pinch on his toe.

"Ouch!" he cried. "Stop that pinching,
Mole. Just because someone pinches you,
you do not have to pinch me!"

"I did not touch you," said Mole.

"You did! You did! You *did!*" cried Troll.

"There is no one else around!"

"Look, Troll, it is too nice a day for arguing," said Mole. "Let's enjoy the sea and forget this silliness."

So they sat and enjoyed the sea. The salt mist touched them and felt cool. Sea gulls flew by, and everything was calm.

Then Mole cried out, "Yikes!" because
someone pinched him in a very pinchy
place.
"You did it again, you fuzzy Troll!"
he shouted.

Troll felt a pinch, too.

"It was *you!*" he shouted back. "This time you pinched me so hard, you made a little red lump. Look!"

Mole looked, and there was a little red lump.

"I did not do that," he said. "You have a hive."

"How can I have just *one* hive!" shouted Troll. "Hives come in bunches!"

"I don't know," shouted Mole, "but you do!"

"All right," said Troll. "We will sit very still with our hands on our heads and *see* which one is pinching."

"You are sneaky," said Mole, "because then you will pinch with your feet."

"Then we will sit very still with our
hands on our heads and our feet in plain
sight."

"Okay, Troll, we will do that. But I am
sitting on seaweed to protect myself on
all sides."

"Then so am I," said Troll.

So they sat very still on big seaweed
piles, with their hands on their heads and
their feet in plain sight to see who was
pinching.

They sat like that for a long time.

"Troll," said Mole at last, "it is too still. Nothing is happening. There is something funny about this."

Someone else thought it was funny, too.

Someone else giggled very loudly. It was a big crab. He had been doing the pinching. They looked so silly that he could not help giggling.

Mole and Troll chased him. But he ran into a tight hole and giggled for half an hour.

"Mole," said Troll, "I am sorry for
shouting at you."
"Me, too," said Mole. "And I would never
pinch you, because you are my friend."
"Me, too," said Troll.
Then they went swimming in a place
where there were no crabs at all.

THE SHOELACES

One day the new spring greens were on
the trees, and Mole had on new shoes.

"Troll," he called. "Yoo-hoo, Troll. I have
new shoes. Aren't they the best shoes
you've ever seen?"

"They are keen," said Troll. "But why
don't you tie the laces?"

"I don't know how."

"Here is how," said Troll.

He tied the laces in a neat bow.

"Thank you very much," said Mole.

"Don't mention it," said Troll. "Now we can stroll through the mushroom fields."

Mole and Troll strolled through the
sunny mushroom fields. Mole looked down
to admire his new shoes in the sun. The
laces were untied.

"Troll," he said.

"Yes, Mole?"

"Will you do me a little favor?"

"Anything."

"Will you tie my laces again? They have come untied from strolling."

Mole sat down on a mushroom cap, and Troll tied the laces in a neat bow.

"There," he said. "Now we can finish our stroll."

"Oh, thank you," said Mole.

"Don't mention it," said Troll.

They had gone just a little farther when —bump! Mole tripped on his shoelaces and fell down flat.

"Are you all right?" asked Troll.

"Fine," said Mole. "But will you do me a little favor?"

"Sure."

"Will you tie my laces? They have come untied again."

"I would love to tie them again," said Troll.

Mole sat down on a shiny stone, and
Troll tied the laces in a nice, neat bow.
"Thank you, Troll," said Mole.
"I wish you wouldn't mention it," said
Troll. He was getting cross.

Then they went through a foxtail patch.
Mole was making a pair of weed scissors
when—boink! He tripped and tumbled
into a pile of foxtails.
"Ouch!" he cried.
"Are you all right?" asked Troll.

"Just dandy," grumbled Mole. "But these laces are not all right. They are dangerous. Will you please tie them *tight?*"

Troll was very vexed.

He said, "I am not a shoe clerk. I am a troll. Why should I tie laces all day long when I do not even wear shoes! *You* tie the laces!"

So Mole tied the laces. He tied them and
tied them and tied them. In fact, he
really knotted them in a triple clove-hitch
knot.

"There," he said. "Now they are on good
and tight."

"Yes," said Troll. "Now they are on
forever."

Mole looked worried.

"Forever?" he said.

"Forever," said Troll. "A triple clove-hitch knot is the same as forever."

"Will I have to wear my shoes in the bathtub?" asked Mole.

"Yes," said Troll.

"In bed?"

"Yes."

"At the *beach*?" asked Mole.

"Forever," said Troll.

Mole burst out crying. He liked his new shoes. But he did not want them on FOREVER.

Just then a robin hopped by. She had
been eyeing the laces for some time.
"Pretty nifty shoelaces you got there,"
she said.
"They are all knotted up!" cried Mole.
"Who wants them!"

"I do," said the robin, "for my nest."

"Then take them!" cried Mole.

The robin untied the laces easily and flew
off singing. She left the shoes.

And Mole and Troll strolled home
happily.

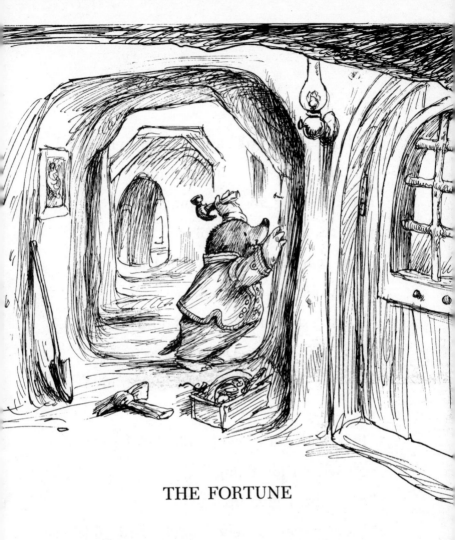

THE FORTUNE

Mole was busy scritching and scratching
and bumping and thumping.

"What's going on?" asked Troll, who lived upstairs. "I hear scritching and scratching and bumping and thumping. All my pictures are going crooked."

"You will never guess what I am doing," said Mole.

"Making an earthquake," said Troll.

"No," said Mole. "Do you give up?"

"No," said Troll. "I do not like to give up."

"Please give up," said Mole, "so I can tell you what I am doing."

"All right. I give up."

"I am making a new tunnel," said Mole. "Come and see."

Mole took Troll through his tunnel. It
had many false doors. And false windows.
And dead ends. And turnabouts. It was
curvy. And swervy. And fat. And thin.

Once Troll almost got stuck.

"This is a beautiful tunnel, Mole," said
Troll. "A bit skimpy in places, but
beautiful."

"I bet you can't make a tunnel like this,"
said Mole.

"Sure I can. I am going home to make a
better tunnel. I will call when it is
ready."

Troll went home and went to work.
Downstairs, Mole heard scritching and
scratching and bumping and thumping
and BASHING and CRASHING!
"Mole!" Troll called out suddenly.
Mole rushed upstairs.

"Is it ready so soon?" he asked.

"No."

"Then why did you call?"

"I was lonesome," said Troll. "And also I needed someone to help me up. I worked so hard that I have spoiled my best suit. I have bashed my plates. I have crashed my crystal ball. Now I am very tired."

"But where is the tunnel?" asked Mole.

"There," said Troll, pointing to a little

dent in the floor. "There is the tunnel."

"That is a dent," said Mole.

"No, that is a tunnel," said Troll, "a small

one. Trolls are no good at digging
tunnels. Trolls are good at telling
fortunes. But not without a crystal ball."
Troll was too sad to say more. Mole
felt sorry.

"I just remembered something," he said.
Mole rushed downstairs. He got an old
lightbulb, forty-five watts, burned out and
pinging inside.
"This will make a fine crystal ball," he
thought, "even if it is not real crystal."
He wrapped the lightbulb in gay party
paper. Then he rushed upstairs again.

"Here, Troll. This is for you," he said.

"What is it? asked Troll.

"Guess," said Mole.

"A fat pickle."

"No. Do you give up?"

"No," said Troll. "I do not like to give
up."

"Then open it."

"Oh!" shouted Troll. "Just what I need most in the world—an old lightbulb!"

"It is a forty-five-watt crystal ball," said Mole.

"You are right," said Troll. "I was holding it upside down. It has a nice ping to it. It makes me happy again. It makes me so happy that now I will read your fortune."

"What does it say?" cried Mole.

"Ping!"

"And what else?"

"Ping! Ping!"

"Very nice," said Mole. "But what does it mean?"

"It means 'Mole will always have a good friend upstairs,'" said Troll.

"And who will my good friend be?" asked Mole.

"Guess," said Troll.

KEY WORDS

bouquet   pinch
chintz   scarecrow
crystal   scissors
hammock   shoelaces
knot   skimpy
lonesome   tunnel
mistake   volunteer